For Phil
—J.B.

Ω

Published by
PEACHTREE PUBLISHERS
1700 Chattahoochee Avenue
Atlanta, Georgia 30318-2112
www.peachtree-online.com

Text and illustrations © 2009 by John Butler
First published in Great Britain by Penguin Books in 2009
First United States edition published in 2009 by Peachtree Publishers

Artwork created in acrylic and colored pencil.

Printed and bound in Singapore
10 9 8 7 6 5 4 3 2 1
First Edition

Library of Congress Cataloging-in-Publication Data

Butler, John, 1952-
Bedtime in the jungle / [written and illustrated by] John Butler. -- 1st ed.
p. cm.
Summary: As dusk falls in the jungle, animal babies and their parents prepare for bedtime.
ISBN 978-1-56145-486-0 / 1-56145-486-9
[1. Stories in rhyme. 2. Bedtime--Fiction 3. Jungle animals--Fiction. 4. Counting--Fiction.] I. Title.
PZ8.3.B9788It 2009
[E]--dc22
2008040592

www.johnbutlerart.com

Bedtime
in the
Jungle

John Butler

PEACHTREE
ATLANTA

It was **sunset**
in the jungle,

And the **sky** was
streaked with **red**.

The **animals**
were **calling**.

It was nearly
time for bed…

It was bedtime
in the jungle,

And the **day** was
almost **done**.

A **rhino** lay
down quietly

Next to her baby
one.

"Sleep," said her mother.

"I'll sleep," said the one.

And they slept in the jungle, as the day was almost done.

It was **bedtime**
in the jungle,

And the **stream** was
shining **blue**.

A **monkey**
made a bed

For her babies
two.

2

"Rest," said their mother.

"We'll rest," said the two.

And they rested in their bed, by the **stream** shining **blue.**

It was **bedtime**
in the jungle,

And **beneath a**
shady **tree**

A **leopard**
tucked her **paws**

Around her babies
three.

"Snuggle," said their mother.

"We'll snuggle," said the three.

And they snuggled up together, beneath the shady tree.

It was **bedtime**
in the jungle,

And the **sun**
glowed no more.

A **wolf**
nuzzled noses

With her babies
four.

4

"Nestle," said their mother.

"We'll nestle," said the four.

And they nestled in their den, as the sun glowed no more.

It was **bedtime**
in the jungle,

And the **moon**
would soon arrive.

A **tiger**
gently licked

All her babies
five.

5

"Quiet," said their mother.

"We'll be quiet," said the five.

And they slowly closed their eyes,
as the moon would soon arrive.

It was **bedtime**
in the jungle,

And in a **nest**
of sticks

A **peahen** smoothed
the feathers

Of her babies
six.

6

"Hush," said their mother.

"We'll hush," said the six.

And they hushed side by side, in their nest made of sticks.

It was **bedtime**
in the jungle,

And the stars shone
in heaven.

A wild pig
snuffled softly

Round her babies
seven.

"Settle," said their mother.

"We'll settle," said the seven.

And they all settled down, as the stars shone in heaven.

It was **bedtime**
in the jungle,

And the **hour** was
getting **late**.

A **duck**
gave kisses

To her babies
eight.

8

"Cuddle," said their mother.

"We'll cuddle," said the eight.

And they cuddled close to Mama, as the hour was getting late.

It was bedtime
in the jungle,

And the moon
began to shine.

A crocodile
was lazing

With her babies
nine.

"Snooze," said their mother.

"We'll snooze," said the nine.

And they all snoozed together, as the moon began to shine.

It was **bedtime**
in the jungle,

And by the
river bend

Elephants were
gathering

With their babies
ten.

10

It was nighttime
in the jungle,

And the moon shone
full and bright.

All the
jungle babies

Were safely
sleeping tight.